T A K E   I T   A P A R T
FIRE ENGINE

By Chris Oxlade

Illustrated by Mike Grey

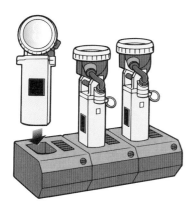
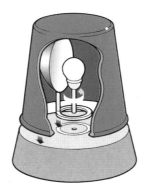
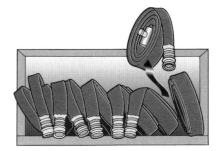

🌸 Belitha Press

First published in the UK in 1998 by

Belitha Press Limited, London House,
Great Eastern Wharf, Parkgate Road,
London SW11 4NQ

ISBN 1 85561 808 7

British Library Cataloguing in Publication
Data for this book is available from the
British Library.

Printed in Hong Kong / China

Editor: Claire Edwards
Designer: Guy Callaby
Illustrator: Mike Grey
Researcher: Susie Brooks
Consultants: Elizabeth Atkinson
    and Robin Kerrod

We should like to thank the West Yorkshire
Fire Service and Angloco Ltd for their help
with this book.

Inside this Book

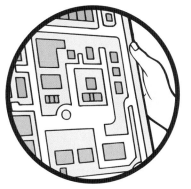

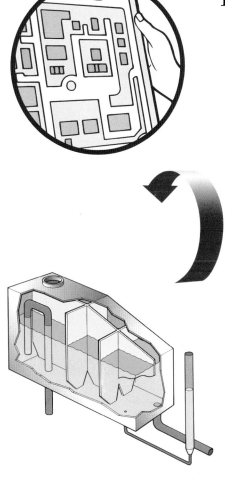

Take a Fire Engine Apart

◕ A fire engine is a truck that helps fire-fighters to put out fires and to deal with other emergencies.

◑ A fire engine has thousands of parts. They are made of metal, plastic, glass and some special fireproof materials.

◕ This book shows you the main parts of a fire engine and how they fit together.

three-piece ladder

Fact box
The first fire engines had no engines to drive them along. They were pulled by horses and the pumps were worked by hand.

water pump

water collecting hose

4

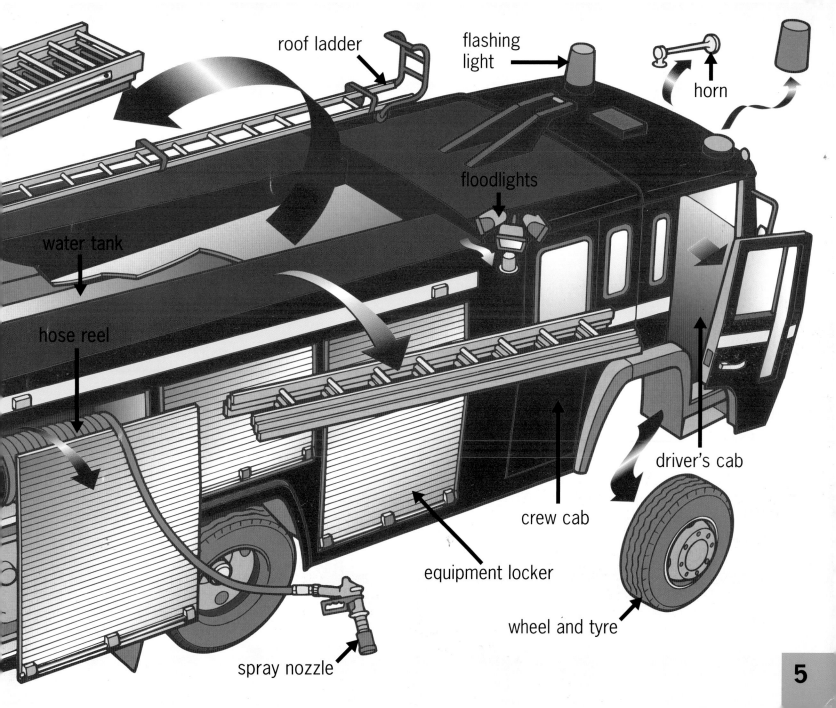

roof ladder

flashing light

horn

floodlights

water tank

hose reel

driver's cab

crew cab

equipment locker

wheel and tyre

spray nozzle

5

The Chassis

- The chassis is a strong frame underneath the engine's body.

- The wheels, suspension, gearbox and engine are all attached to the chassis.

- A powerful diesel engine drives the wheels round and also works the water pump.

- A handle in the cab switches the power from the wheels to the pump.

6-litre diesel engine

front suspension

Power take-off

The engine makes a drive shaft spin round. The drive shaft turns another two shafts from the power take-off. One turns the rear (back) wheels. The other turns the pump.

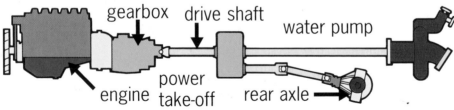

gearbox   drive shaft

water pump

engine   power take-off   rear axle

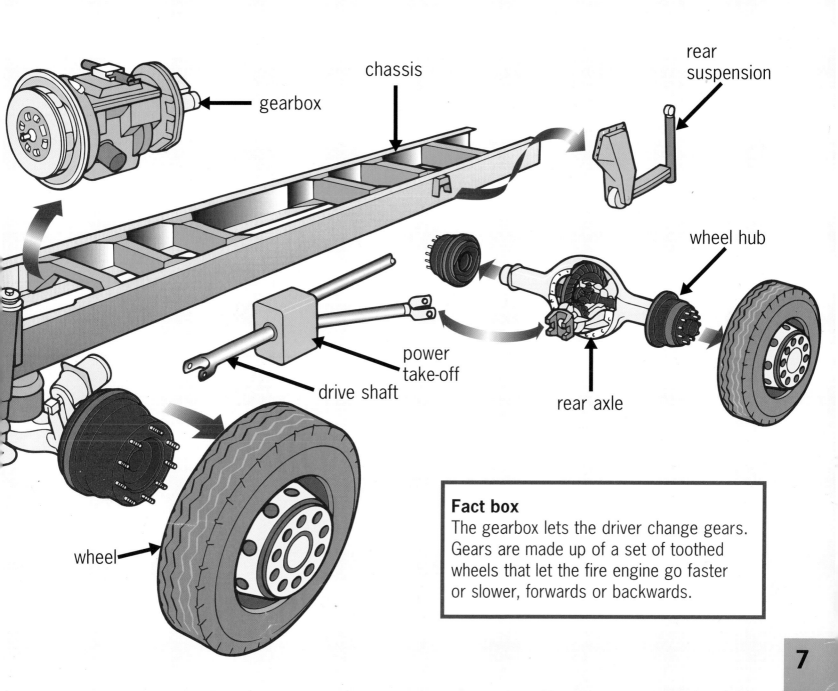

gearbox

chassis

rear suspension

wheel hub

power take-off

drive shaft

rear axle

wheel

Fact box

The gearbox lets the driver change gears. Gears are made up of a set of toothed wheels that let the fire engine go faster or slower, forwards or backwards.

The Body

⊖ The fire engine's body is attached to the chassis. It comes in two parts, the cab and the rear body.

⊖ The cab is where the fire-fighters sit.

⊘ The rear body carries the fire-fighting equipment and a huge tank of water.

⊖ The body is made from a strong metal frame covered in thin metal panels.

Fact box
The metal used to make and cover the frame is aluminium, which does not go rusty when it gets wet.

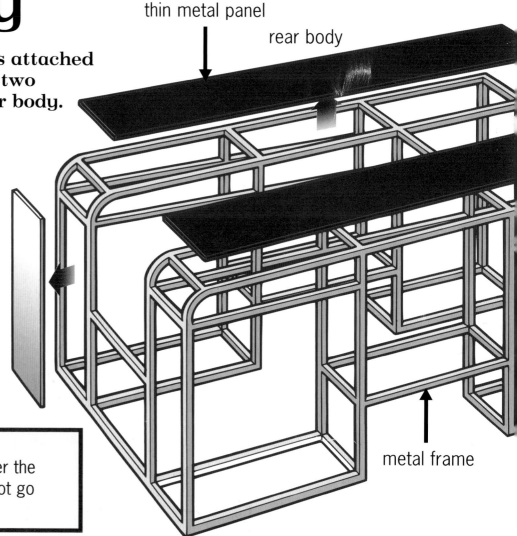

thin metal panel

rear body

metal frame

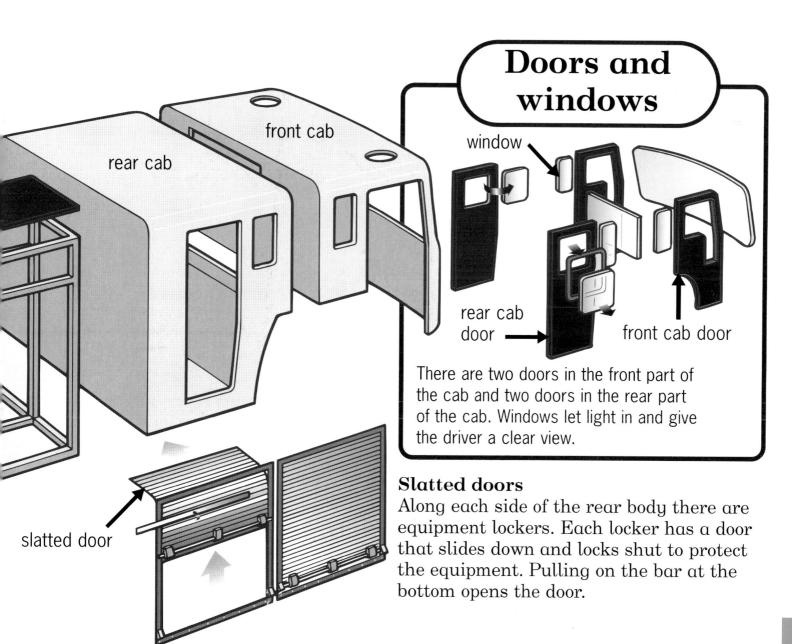

rear cab

front cab

slatted door

Doors and windows

window

rear cab door

front cab door

There are two doors in the front part of the cab and two doors in the rear part of the cab. Windows let light in and give the driver a clear view.

Slatted doors

Along each side of the rear body there are equipment lockers. Each locker has a door that slides down and locks shut to protect the equipment. Pulling on the bar at the bottom opens the door.

9

In the Cab

⊘ The cab is divided into two parts. The front part is just like the cab of an ordinary truck.

⊘ The rear part of the cab has room for four fire-fighters.

⊘ As well as driving controls, there are controls for some of the equipment, including the flood lamps and water pump.

⊘ Soft padding on the sharp corners protects the fire-fighters from a bumpy ride.

Fact box
In the early 1900s fire engines had no cabs. The crew stood on planks along the side of the engine and held on tightly.

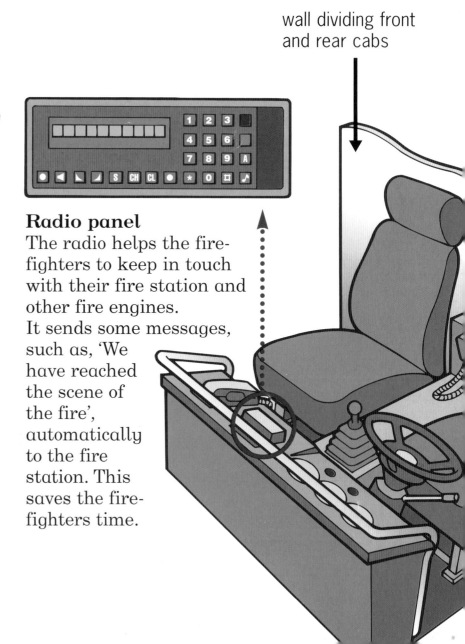

wall dividing front and rear cabs

Radio panel
The radio helps the fire-fighters to keep in touch with their fire station and other fire engines.
It sends some messages, such as, 'We have reached the scene of the fire', automatically to the fire station. This saves the fire-fighters time.

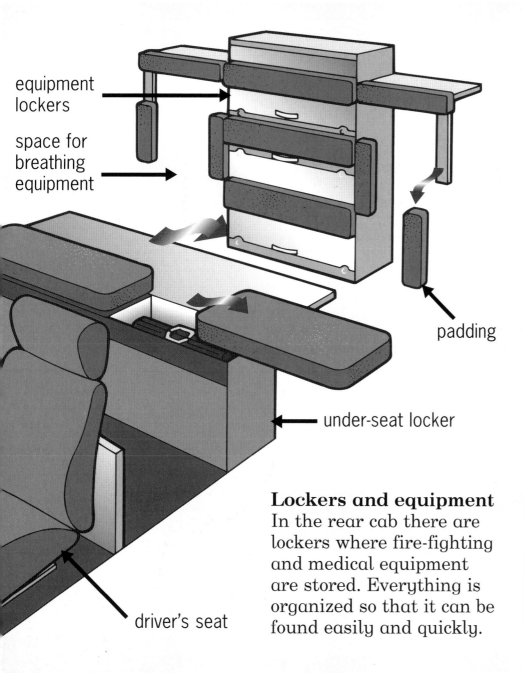

equipment lockers

space for breathing equipment

padding

under-seat locker

driver's seat

Lockers and equipment
In the rear cab there are lockers where fire-fighting and medical equipment are stored. Everything is organized so that it can be found easily and quickly.

Clear maps

The fire engine carries maps that help the fire-fighters find the scene of the fire quickly. Some maps show buildings where there are hazards, such as dangerous chemicals that could explode.

Light and Sound

⊘ A fire engine has several different lights.

⊘ There are lights to warn drivers on the road that the fire engine is coming.

◉ Other lights are used at the scene of a fire or emergency when it is dark.

◉ A noisy horn also helps to warn other drivers.

Flood lamps

Bright flood lamps are fixed to a telescopic mast on top of the fire engine. When air is pumped into the mast, it rises so that the lamps light up a wide area.

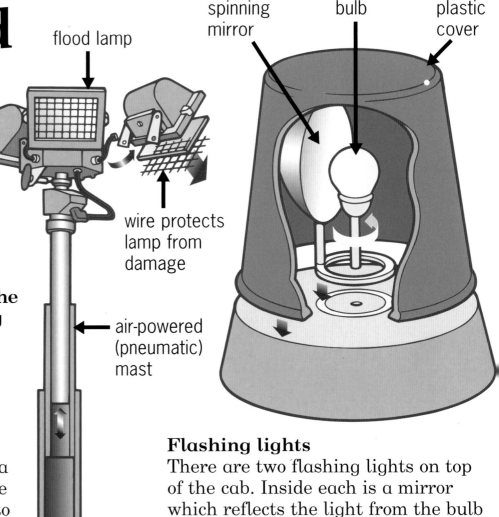

flood lamp

wire protects lamp from damage

air-powered (pneumatic) mast

spinning mirror

bulb

plastic cover

Flashing lights

There are two flashing lights on top of the cab. Inside each is a mirror which reflects the light from the bulb to make a thin beam. As the mirror spins round, it makes the light flash.

Horn

The horn is very loud. It works a bit like a trumpet. Air is pumped through it by an air pump inside the fire engine.

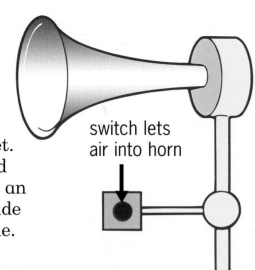

switch lets air into horn

Portable generator

This portable generator makes electricity for portable floodlights when lights are needed away from the fire engine.

fuel tank

engine turns generator

Hand torches

Each fire-fighter has a torch to use inside dark or smoky buildings. The torches have rechargeable batteries. They are stored in a recharging station inside the cab.

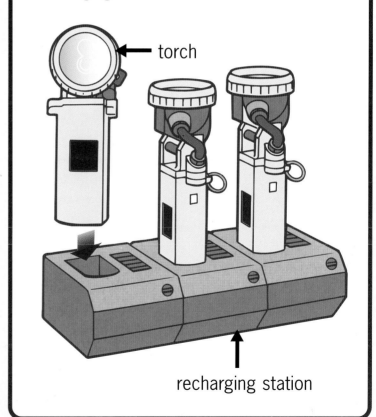

torch

recharging station

Getting Water

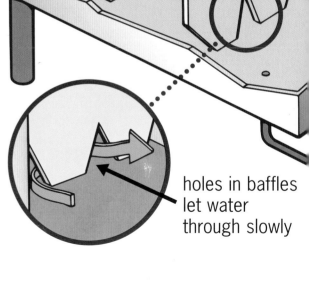

air hole

pipe for filling tank

🔩 Fire-fighters normally use water to put out a fire. Here you can see where the water comes from.

🔩 There is a huge tank of water inside the fire engine. There is enough water inside it to put out small fires.

🔩 The fire engine can also get water from the mains water supply under the street or from nearby rivers, lakes or canals.

holes in baffles let water through slowly

Fact box
If there were no baffles in the water tank, the sloshing water could make the fire engine topple over.

Baffles
Walls called baffles inside the water tank stop the water sloshing about as the fire engine drives to the fire.

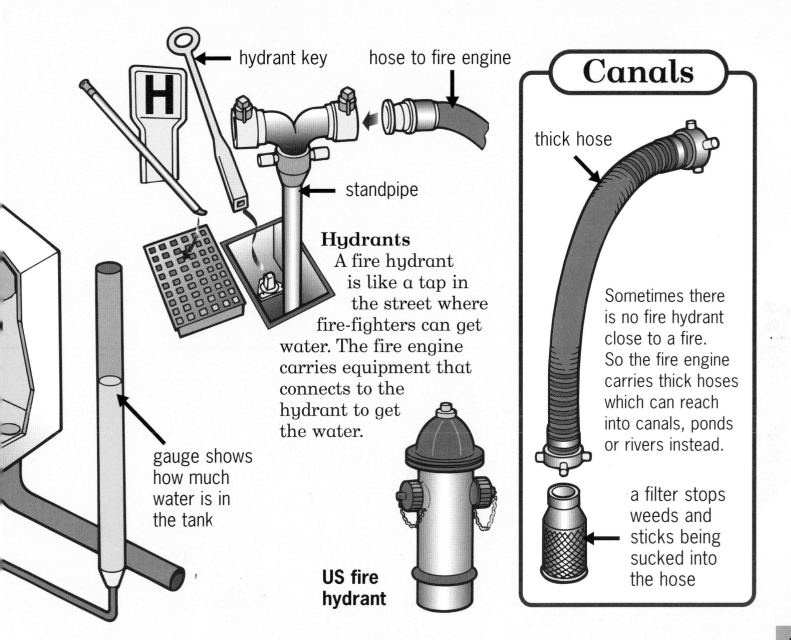

hydrant key

hose to fire engine

H

standpipe

Hydrants

A fire hydrant is like a tap in the street where fire-fighters can get water. The fire engine carries equipment that connects to the hydrant to get the water.

gauge shows how much water is in the tank

US fire hydrant

Canals

thick hose

Sometimes there is no fire hydrant close to a fire. So the fire engine carries thick hoses which can reach into canals, ponds or rivers instead.

a filter stops weeds and sticks being sucked into the hose

Pumping Water

- ◐ **The fire engine has a water pump that pumps water to the fire.**

- ◐ **The pump is worked by the power take-off from the engine.**

- ◐ **The pump sucks water from the water tank or from a hydrant, canal or river.**

- ◐ **It pushes the water along hoses to the fire.**

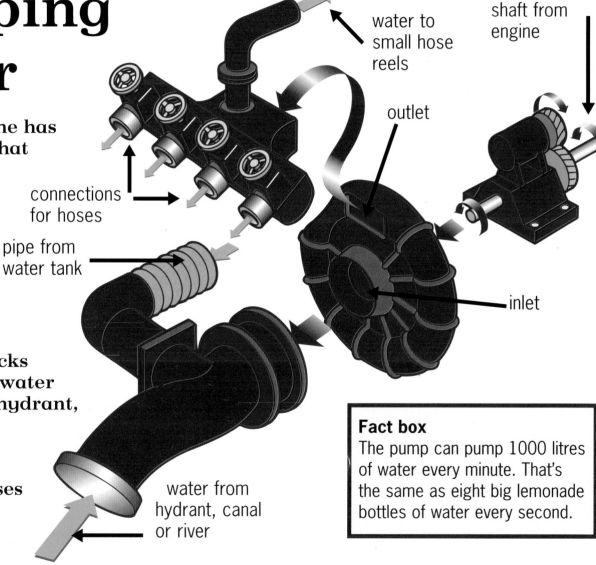

water to small hose reels

power take-off shaft from engine

outlet

connections for hoses

pipe from water tank

inlet

water from hydrant, canal or river

Fact box
The pump can pump 1000 litres of water every minute. That's the same as eight big lemonade bottles of water every second.

Pump controls

The pump is controlled by levers. Gauges show how much water it is pumping and if it is working properly.

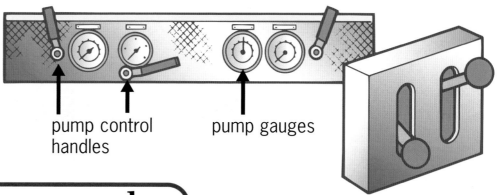

pump control handles

pump gauges

How the pump works

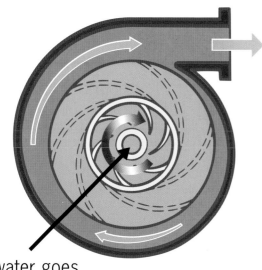

water goes into inlet

water comes out of outlet

The pump spins round very fast, throwing water from the middle of the pump to the outside. This sucks water from the inlet into the middle and pushes it out of the outlets.

Portable pump

Some fires happen in places where the fire engine cannot reach. When this happens, the fire-fighters use a portable pump to pump the water to the fire.

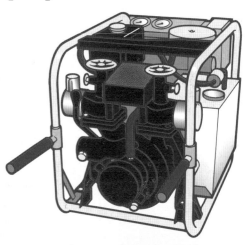

Water Hoses

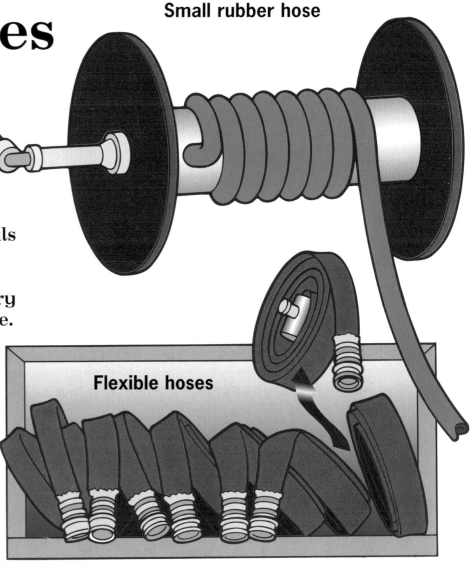

Small rubber hose

Flexible hoses

● A hose is a long, bendy tube which carries water from place to place. Some fire engines have up to 20 hoses.

● There are hoses to carry water from fire hydrants, canals or rivers, to the water pump.

● There are more hoses to carry water from the pump to the fire.

● Small hoses are made of thin rubber. Large hoses are thicker and made of fabric.

Fact box
If a hose gets a hole in it and starts leaking, the fire-fighters wrap a piece of cloth called a hose bandage around it.

18

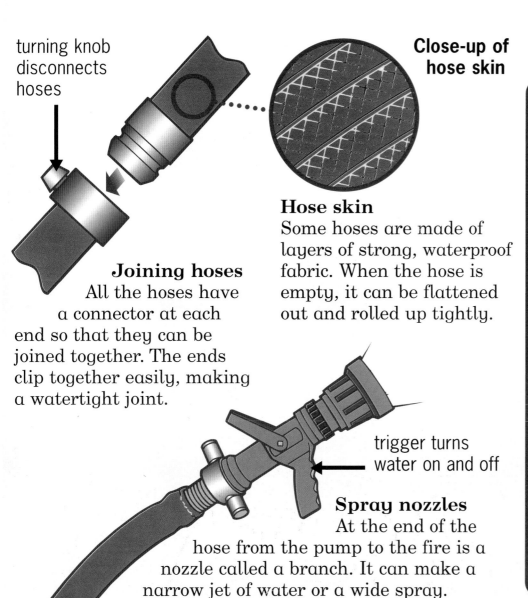

turning knob
disconnects
hoses

Close-up of hose skin

Hose skin
Some hoses are made of layers of strong, waterproof fabric. When the hose is empty, it can be flattened out and rolled up tightly.

Joining hoses
All the hoses have a connector at each end so that they can be joined together. The ends clip together easily, making a watertight joint.

trigger turns water on and off

Spray nozzles
At the end of the hose from the pump to the fire is a nozzle called a branch. It can make a narrow jet of water or a wide spray.

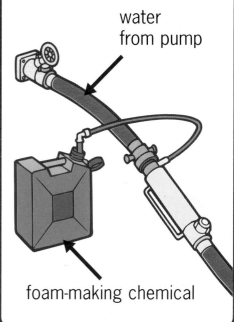

Foam hoses

Sometimes fire-fighters spray foam on to a fire instead of water. The foam is made by mixing water with special chemicals.

water from pump

foam-making chemical

Climbing In

13.5 metre ladder

⊘ The fire engine carries several ladders which the fire-fighters use to climb up the outside of buildings.

⊘ The main ladder is telescopic. It has three sections which slide in and out of each other.

⊘ There is also a short extension ladder and a roof ladder.

⊘ The ladders are stored on the fire engine's roof.

Fact box
The main ladder here is 13.5 metres long. It can reach the top of a four-storey building.

pole helps to push ladder up side of house

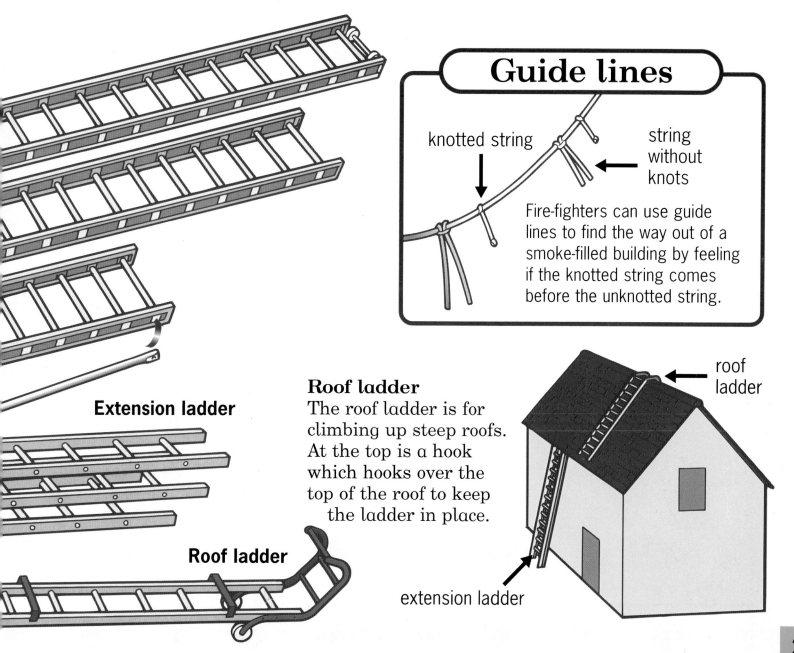

Guide lines

knotted string

string without knots

Fire-fighters can use guide lines to find the way out of a smoke-filled building by feeling if the knotted string comes before the unknotted string.

Extension ladder

Roof ladder

Roof ladder
The roof ladder is for climbing up steep roofs. At the top is a hook which hooks over the top of the roof to keep the ladder in place.

roof ladder

extension ladder

Emergency Kit

⊘ Fire engines carry equipment to help with emergencies such as car crashes as well as fires.

⊖ Most of the emergency equipment is for cutting metal and lifting heavy objects.

⊖ The fire engine also has a first-aid kit in the cab. It includes oxygen to help people who have breathed in smoke, and special equipment for treating burns.

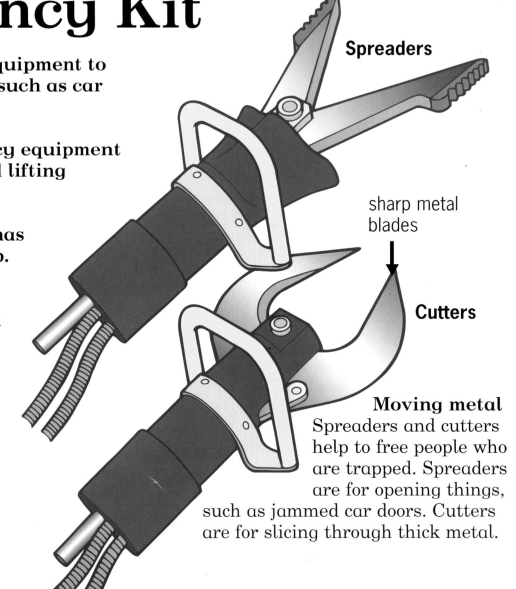

Spreaders

sharp metal blades

Cutters

Fact box
Fire-fighters can cut the roof off a car in under a minute using powerful hydraulic cutters.

Moving metal
Spreaders and cutters help to free people who are trapped. Spreaders are for opening things, such as jammed car doors. Cutters are for slicing through thick metal.

Hydraulics

The spreaders and cutters are worked by hydraulics. Liquid is pumped into a cylinder, pushing a piston outwards with great force. The piston moves the blades of the cutters and spreaders.

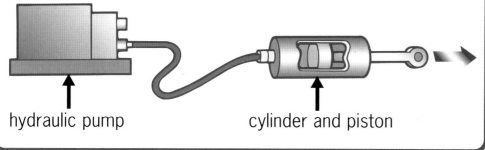

hydraulic pump

cylinder and piston

Hand winch

This winch can lift or pull heavy objects, such as a car up a steep slope. A fire-fighter moves the handle backwards and forwards, which pulls the strong steel rope through the winch.

Thermal camera

When a fire-fighter looks through this special camera, he or she sees a bright spot where there is any hot or warm object. The camera helps fire-fighters to find people in dark, smoke-filled buildings.

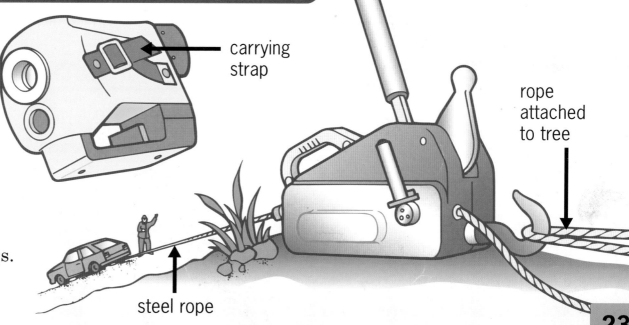

carrying strap

handle

rope attached to tree

steel rope

Fire-fighter's Clothing

helmet

jacket

🔩 Fire-fighters wear special clothes which help to protect them from the smoke and heat.

🔩 They have long trousers called salopettes and a thick jacket made of fireproof material.

🔩 A helmet protects the fire-fighter from falling objects.

🔩 The fire-fighters put on special clothes in the fire engine's cab as they rush to the fire.

salopettes

boots

Fact box
Fire-fighters sometimes wear a special thick rubber glove to stop themselves getting an electric shock.

Chemical suit

There are sometimes dangerous chemicals at the scene of a fire. Chemical oversuits protect the fire-fighters from chemicals which might harm their skin.

← chemical oversuit

bottle of air

Breathing apparatus

Before fire-fighters go into a smoke-filled building, they put on breathing apparatus. It lets them breathe clean air instead of choking smoke.

Getting dressed

1 Fire-fighter's clothing is ready in the cab.

2 He puts his feet into his boots.

3 He begins to pull up his salopettes.

4 He puts the straps over his shoulders.

5 His puts on his fireproof jacket.

6 He pulls on his breathing apparatus.

Tall Ladders

⊘ On these pages you can see a different type of fire engine. It has a long telescopic ladder.

⊘ The ladder can reach high into the air and swivel from side to side.

⊘ A fire-fighter can spray water on to the fire from the platform at the top of the ladder.

⊘ The ladder can also be used to rescue people from tall buildings.

Turntable

The ladder sits on top of a turntable on the back of the fire engine. It can swing right round to reach buildings to the side of the engine. There are controls on the turntable for turning and extending the ladder. The ladder is worked by hydraulics.

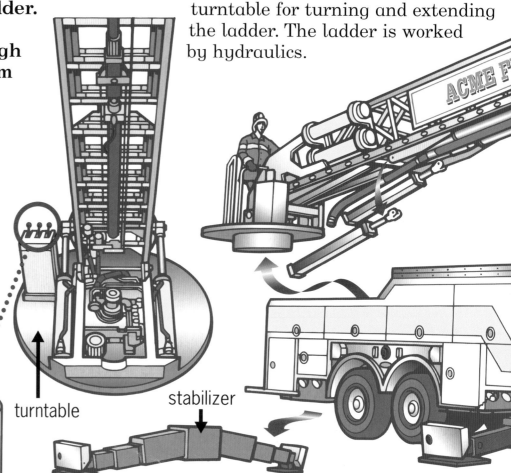

turntable and ladder controls

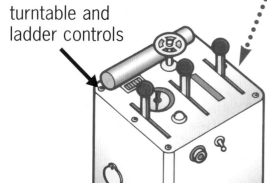

turntable

stabilizer

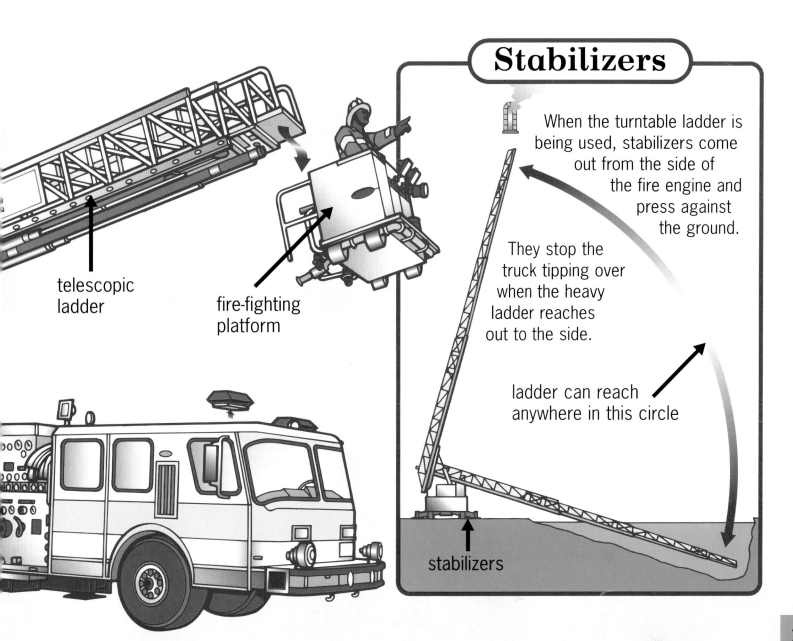

Stabilizers

telescopic
ladder

fire-fighting
platform

When the turntable ladder is
being used, stabilizers come
out from the side of
the fire engine and
press against
the ground.

They stop the
truck tipping over
when the heavy
ladder reaches
out to the side.

ladder can reach
anywhere in this circle

stabilizers

Special Fire Engines

◉ On these pages you can find out about some special fire engines.

◉ Some help to fight fires in places where normal fire engines cannot reach.

◉ Some are designed to fight just one sort of fire.

Tracked fire engine
This fire engine has tracks instead of wheels. It can drive over rough and rocky ground. Tracked fire engines fight moorland and forest fires.

Airport fire truck
Every airport has its own fire engines. If an aircraft crashes, the fire engine sprays foam over it to stop it catching fire.

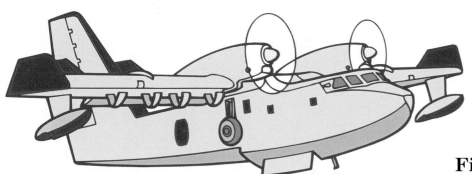

Fire-fighting plane

This plane is used to fight forest fires. It skims across a lake, scooping water into its water tank. Then it flies over a forest fire and dumps the water on to the flames.

Fact box

Helicopters can also fight fires. They scoop up water in a huge cloth bucket that hangs underneath, and tip the water over the fire.

Fire-fighting boat

This boat is like a floating fire engine. It fights fires in docks or along river banks. It sucks water from the sea or the river and sprays it on to the fire.

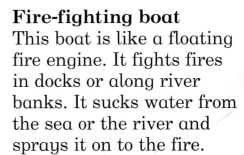

Useful Terms

axle A rod that carries a vehicle's wheels. The wheels spin round on the axle.

breathing apparatus Equipment to help someone breathe, made up of a mask and an oxygen supply.

cab The space at the front a fire engine or lorry where the driver and crew sit.

chassis The strong frame of a vehicle that supports its body. The engine and wheels are attached to the chassis.

cylinder A tube inside which a piston moves up and down.

diesel engine A type of engine that burns diesel fuel inside its cylinders to make it work.

drive shaft A rod that is turned by an engine to make wheels or other parts of a machine turn too.

extension An extra part that is added to an object to make it larger or longer.

filter A sheet of material with tiny holes in it. It lets water pass through, but not larger objects.

gauge A device that measures quantity, or how high or low something is.

generator A machine that makes electricity when its shaft is spun round quickly.

hazard Anything that might be dangerous.

hydrant An outlet from an underground water pipe, usually made up of a pipe and a tap-like part to which a hose can be fitted.

hydraulic A hydraulic machine works when oil is pumped into its cylinders.

nozzle A narrow hole at the end of a hose. When water goes through a nozzle it forms a narrow jet or a wide spray.

piston A part that moves up and down in a cylinder, to move something else.

pneumatic A pneumatic machine works when air is pumped into it.

portable A portable object is one designed to be carried round, so it can be used anywhere.

power take-off A part of a fire engine's drive shaft that sends power to the fire engine's water pump instead of its wheels.

pump A machine that sucks water in one end and forces it out at the other.

rechargeable Something that can have power put back into it is rechargeable.

shaft A rod that spins round, turning anything that is fixed to it.

stabilizer Something that helps to stop a vehicle tipping up.

standpipe A vertical pipe, attached to a water outlet that helps to control the pressure of the water.

suspension Springs that connect the wheels to the chassis. Suspension softens the effect of bumps in the road on the vehicle.

telescopic A ladder or mast that has several sections that slide in and out of each other to make it longer or shorter.

thermal A word used to describe anything to do with heat.

turntable A round table that can turn from side to side. Some fire engines have a ladder on a turntable.

winch A machine that can lift or pull along heavy objects.

Index

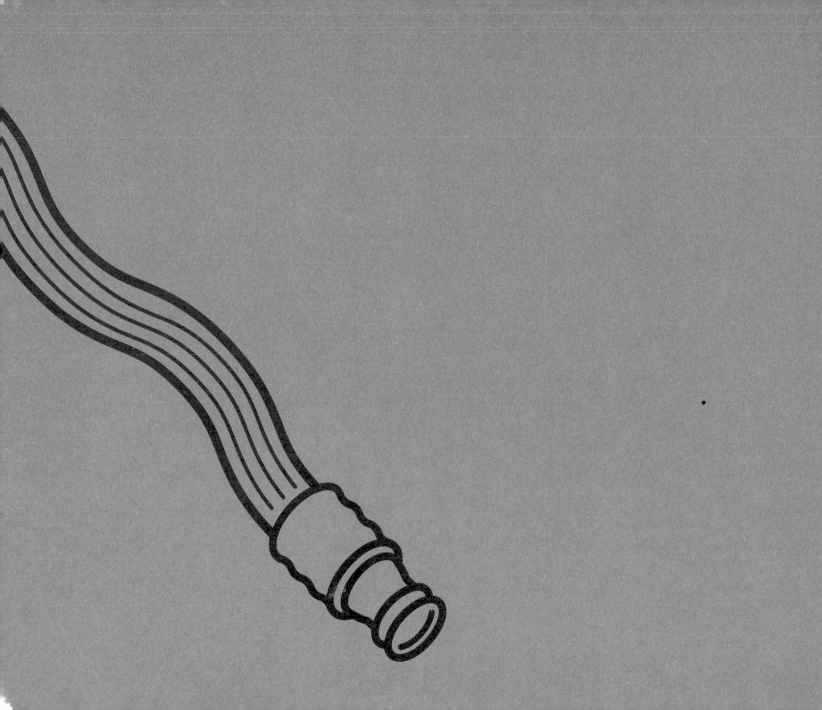